Destiny

Flairs and Glairs

Publication House

"Destiny"

ISBN No: " 978-93-90799-83-1"
1st Edition
Language – English and Hindi

Flairs and Glairs
Publication House
Regd. Under MSME Act.

Disclaimer

This is a work of fiction and solely represent the thoughts of the corresponding authors of the articles. Our editors have tried their best to edit the content of all the authors and check the plagiarism.

All the write-ups in this book are unique and are only published in this book.

In case any plagiarism or error is found, only the author is responsible alone, and not the publisher or the Compilers.

Cover Designing and Book Formatting
Shubham Shah and Ishani Agarwal

Co Author

Shubham Shah (Founder Flairs and Glairs)
Ishani Agarwal (Co-Founder Flairs and Glairs)

1. Mohini Das
2. Swati Wake Shinde
3. Sahina Ghugha
4. Payal
5. Payal Rajpoot
6. Kalpana Mohanta
7. Shushree Arati
8. Priyanka Sharma
9. Ajay Kumar Jena
10. Evinyne Miravite Novena
11. Shazia Jabeen
12. Mahima Lodhi
13. Shaheen Shah
14. Keerthana Hails
15. Sonam Rajput
16. Kiran Mourya
17. Simran Rajpal
18. Vid
19. Shreeja Sathish
20. Jyoti Mourya
21. Ayushi Mishra
22. Madhvi Jha
23. Soniya Varghese
24. Reetika Singh
25. Ruchika Bansal
26. Rinkal N. Dhokiya
27. Samyuktha Sathish
28. Shama Kamra
29. Pooja Gautam

30. Shemila
31. Hema Kirthiga J
32. Harshita (Manu)
33. Krish Balani
34. Sukanya Gunja
35. Shradha Gindlani
36. Pramila Rawat
37. Akanksha Gupta
38. Kiran
39. Priyanka Rawat
40. Mampi Gayan
41. Dia Dey
42. Muskan
43. R.V. Teena
44. Gunwanti Harish
45. Somya Jain
46. Poonam B. Naik
47. Nancy Chaudhry
48. Darshna Karushnaji Gaudkhede

Shubham Shah

(Founder- Flairs and Glairs)

Shubham Shah, an entrepreneur at "Flairs & Glairs" a brand with dynamics in events organizing and cultural educational pan INDIA, is a 26yrs old guy who recently has entered the digital platform of imprinting emotions. He has initiated with his own open mic platform to help budding poets and aspiring writers under his brand named as "Teekhe Zasbaaat"

He is a commerce graduate from the Bhagalpur City of Bihar. He states Writing has impersonated him since childhood and he has now been writing for over a decade!

Cooking, on the other hand, is his passion! He also mentions, trying out new things just tickles him!

When asked sir, Why SPICY EMOTIONS?

He smiled and added, "agar jasbaat teekhe na ho toh wo jasbaat kahan" Spices are all that blends! So do his words!

As a chef, he presents to you his dish! Hot and freshly served! Taste it! Feel it! Enjoy it! You can also find his writing in the Book "Teekhe Zasbaaat" and 50+ Co-authored anthologies. With his passion to explore opportunities across Platforms, he is working with keen devotion and We wish him all the very best for his future ventures.

He is Featured in the International Magazine DeMode for his upcoming solo novel.

He is Approved by Ne8x for its Lit Fest, and is a Golden Star Awards 2020 Winner.

He is a India Book of Records Holder for his Anthology Satrang, and has the Grandmaster title by Asia Book of Records, for the same.

He has also been featured in Prabhat Khabar, Dainik Jagran, and a lot of other Newspapers in Bihar for his achievements.

He has been a proud co-author to

India Book Of Records (Title- Black)

World Book Of Records (Title -15 Wonders of Poetries)

India Book Of Records (Title - Aaina)

Vajra World Records Holder (Title - Gustakhi Maaf Hai)

High Range of Records Holder (Title - Gustakhi Maaf Hai)

Indian Book of Records

(Title - Road from Worst to Best)

Share your reviews on his

INSTAGRAM

@spicy_emotions
@shubham4shah

Or via email on

shubham2shah@gmail.com

To stay tuned to his work and opportunities follow his business Handles

INSTAGRAM   FACEBOOK   YOUTUBE

@flairsandglairs
@teekhezasbaaat

WEBSITE:

https://flairsandglairs.in/
https://flairsandglairs.com/

Ishani Agarwal

(Co-Founder- Flairs and Glairs)

Ishani Agarwal hails from the City of Joy, Kolkata.
She is the co-founder of her Community "Teekhe Zasbaaat" and Flairs and Glairs Publication.
Been a Compiler for 45+ Anthologies, she is in the process for more. Co-authored in 150+ Anthologies. She is a India Book of Records Holder, a Vajra World Records Holder, a High Range of Records Holder, an OMG Book of Records Holder, a Bravo Record holder, a Forever Star Book of World Records and an Indian Book of Records Holder.
Approved by Ne8x for its Lit Fest 2020, and Literary Icon 2020. Also a Golden Star Awards Winner 2020.
She has also been awarded with India Star Republic Award 2021, a part of She Awards by Awards Arc and Winner of Nari Samman 2021 by Literoma.

She is also selected as Best Achiever of the Year by AwardsArc and Most Challenging Compiler Award by Spectrum Awards.
She got her first solo Published,a solo Compilation consisting of first 750 contents of hers, titled "Hand That Burnt While Healing".

She has been featured by the National Magazine "Taree Zameen Par" with the title 'unstoppable'.
Also featured in the International Magazine DeMode for her upcoming solo novel, she is proud to write on social issues, and is happy with the love she is receiving.
Connect with her on Instagram: @Ishani_agarwal_quotes / @compilations_so_far

Mohini Das

Mohini Das, she is 22years old B.A student of Krishna Kanta Handiq State Open University
of Assam. She us from Bongaigaon city of Assam. Now she is doing her part tym job of Doctor's Chamber. She is create a new shayri Channel...... Name of---- The Shayri Cottage

Iss Chote Se Dil Mai Khawahis Bahut Hai
Chote Se Aankhon Mai Sapne Bhi Bade Hai
Na Jane Anewala Pal Kya Dekha De
Khud Ke Dam Pai Kuch Kar Jane Ka Josh Hai

Kya Fark Paddta Hai
Apke Pas Paisa Ho ya Na Ho
Agar Zindegi Mai Ijjat Kamaye Ho To
Paise Bhi Kam Padd Jayenge
Jeb Mai Rakhne Ke Liye

Swati Wake Shinde

Swati Wake Shinde is 27 years old. She is from pune city in Maharashtra. She is a Business woman and dreamer. She want to write real emotions, feelings and most important pain behind smile

झुटा निकला है तू,
मेरे को तड़पानेवाला,
दर्द निकला है तू।
हरपल आँखों को,
रुलानेवाला,
दुख निकला है तू।
प्यारे दिल को तोड़नेवाला,
ओठों से हँसी छिननेवाला,
मेरे जिंदगी का हर सपना,
भुलाने को मजबूर करनेवाला,
मेरे खुशी को जलानेवाला,
और मेरे को बेवफाई का
एहसास करानेवाला,
एक बेवफा शक्स
निकला है तू।
   सच,
बेवफा निकला है तू।।।
एक ही दर्द ले बैठे है,
अपनी ही मंजिल खो बैठे है।
बताऊ तो भी कैसे बताऊ ये दर्द ?
सुनने के लिए उनके पास वक्त नहीं।
दिखाऊ तो भी कैसे दिखाऊ मोहब्बत ?
उनकी मोहब्बत हम नहीं।
चाहके भी चाहू कैसे ?
उनकी चाहत हम नही।
रखू भी तो उम्मीद कैसे रखू उनसे ?
जिनकी उम्मीद हम नही।
हमारी तो जिंदगी है ओ
और हम उनकी जिंदगी नही।

Sahina Ghugha

Sahina Ghugha is 19 year old b.com student at Saurashtra university Rajkot. She is from Jamnagar city of Gujarat. She is state level winner in poetry competition 2017. She is Co-author of 15+ anthologies. She is an amazing writer and poet and she wants do something for society through her pen.
Insta ID:- Itz_Sahina_write

छुपे रुस्तम

माना कयामत लाता है आशिक़ी का ग़म
मगर हो तुम भी छुपके रोने वाले छुपे रुस्तम

जुदाई सही नहीं जाती हमसे ये बात तो बयां किए
पर तड़पते हो तुम भी इससे अनजान थे हम

कुछ लम्हें थे बिखरे से, आज तू समेट ले इन्हें
यादें जो मैं करूं याद, हो जाती है आंखें नम

मिला करते थे तुम पहले बहुत, ज़िद करते थे
आज भी वो याद आती है तुम्हारी दी हुई कसम

जुदा किया भी खुदा ने, दे कर मजबूरियां हज़ारों
वरना कर सके हमें अलग, वो कायनात में कहां दम

रोये तो तुम भी होगे, आंसू बेहद तुमने भी है बहाए
पर जो घाव मिल चुके है, उसका नहीं कोई मरहम

Payal Gehlaut

Myself payal gehlaut
,I am 18 years old nd from Delhi
Insta i'd :- payalgehlaut

Tute se ,bikhre se,pnne h
Aaj nhi to kal sawar jaenge
Tedi si ,medhi si jindagi ek noka h
Apna dam pe paar kar jaenge
Spno k liye hum kai baar apno se bhi lad jaenge
Ab chhote bache thodi h jo akela paakr khud ko dar jaenge
Ha hum bhi insaan h par unme se nhi jo bina kuch kiye hi
mar jaenge
Hunar jo chhupa h andar phchaan k use itihaas nya rach
jaenge
Jindagi hisse me apne kuch hi din ki hui to
Dilo me jgh bna k gujar jaenge
Or mile jada pal to izzat dekr izzat le kr
Khusiyon ka ghr bnaenge
Bhagvan thodi h aakhir me chaar kandho pe svaar hokr hum
bhi is jindagi k jaal se nikal jaenge

Kaise kahu ki kuch nhi mila jindagi me
Jindagi se itni sundar maa mili h
Musibto ki chaabi maano me haath me aa giri h
Meri maa meri khusiyon ki ldi h, meri maa mere liye
bhagwan se bhi bdi h,muskilo me meri vo meri parchaai ban
k khdi h
Meri maa mere saath hai to duniya mera kya kar paegi
Khatra aaya mujhpe to vo mujhse aage khadi paegi
Maa meri devi, durga ,kaali h Bdi muskilo se usne apni
aulad paali h
Jab khu usse ki kuch chahiye to btaao na maa
To list uski hmesha khaali h
Mere liye maine bss abtk use ldte hue dekha h isliye
bhagwan ka drjaa maine use de diya
Ek duje ka dukh hmne saja kar liya
Mrte dam tk saath nibhane ka wada kar diya
Maine meri maa ki har dard mitane ka irada kr liya
Is jindagi ko maine maa k hwale har diya

Payal Rajpoot

My name is payal 19 years old pursuing BCA. I am from Delhi and writing is my passion . I am co-author in 4 books.
And I want to be an author so that I would be able to express my feelings towards society and others .
Insta ID:- Dileshayerana

ज़िन्दगी

ये किस मोड़ पर आ पहुंची है जिंदगी,

यहाँ आने का कोई इरादा तो न था

क्या वजह है जो आज खाली सी हूँ ,

किस्मत से माँगा कुछ ज्यादा तो न था

न जाने क्यों गुमराह सी हो गई हूँ

किस अनजाने मंजर पर आकर खो गई हूँ

जागकर ही तो निकली थी सपनों को साथ लिए

पर अब इन सपनों में ही सो गई हूँ

क्या मंजिल मुझसे दूर हो गई है ..

या मैंने खुद मंजिल को दूर कर लिया है ...

चाहतें क्या थी मेरी, और क्या किस्मत ने मुझे दिया है

मैं सवालों के जवाब ढूंढती आज खुद सवाल सी बन कर रह गई हूँ ,

जिस नदी के खिलाफ कश्ती चलाई थी मैंने आज उसी की लहरों के साथ बह गई हूँ।

ढूंढ रही हूँ खुद के अस्तित्व को जानूँ तो के क्या गलती मेरी है ..

मैं ही देख नही पा रही हूँ या मेरी राह अंधेरी है

क्या कारण है जो मैं आगे बढ़ नही पा रही हूँ,

कौन सी राह है ये जिसपर में चलती जा रही हूँ।

ए जिंदगी क्या वजह है जो तू थका रही है ,

जो मैं जानना नही चाहती वो तू मुझे क्यों बता रही है

ये दोष मेरे कर्मो का है

या मेरी किस्मत मुझे सता रही है।।

 पर मेरी भी सुन ले के जिंदगी

तेरे पास तजुर्बा है तो मेरे पास जस्बा है

खुशी सी है तू

गम सी हूँ मैं

यकीन है कि एक दिन बीत ही जाऊँगी

तू प्रयास कर मुझे हराने के,

यकीन है खुद पर की एक दिन में जीत ही जाउंगी ।।

Kalpana Mohanta

kalpana mohanta is 20 year old GNM nursing student of Biju Patnaik nursing training school Baripada, Mayurbhanj . Recently she have started writing poems and she wants do something for society through her pen.

-Wakt Ki Ahmiyat):-

Wakt kisiki liye
Nehi rukta   Likin..!!?
Ye tumhare liye ruk jayegi?
Wakt kehti hai ki
Mein fir aaunga..
Kya patah tujhe hasanga ya..
Rula dunga.
Jina hai toh iss pal mein ji le
Kyunki__?
Agle pal mere bas mein nehi..
Mein chala jaunga.

Aye Meri Zindigi

Meri Zindagi..
Sayad mujhse udass hai
Mujhe manna-na v nehi aata..
Kya karun??
Aye zindagi
tu kyun udaas hai?
Mein hun naa
Tujhe fir se muskurana Sikha dunga
Fir tu mujhe yaad karegi
Oye meri jaan
Tera shukriya..

Sushre Aarati

Sushree Arati Pattniak is a dreamer, a New writer.Hails from Ganjam, Odisha. She's a Teacher by profession and a writer by passion.   She loves to do things in her own way uniquly. Her mind is very creative.she used different innovative ideas in her work. Shushree's writing always sparkled in regional magazines (Odia), She has written numbers of poem for various magazine and a notable author of Pritipanati E - Magazine, Aawahan and Sudhapallab. And her relationship with Pen and Paper is growing strongly. The amount of love she pouring to the writing the equal amount of love and credit showering on her. Eventually she is going to make an impact in the writing world.

तुम चुनो तो सही....
लडखडायेगें पेर बार बार...
तुम इक कदम पहले निकालो तो सही...
फिर गिरना, फिर उठना तुम..
पहले राहों में तुम चलो तो सही ।।
जिंदगी की कसती है, डगमगायेगा जरूर
तुम इक बार सम्भालने की कोशिश करो तो सही..
उस अंधी, वो तूफान का सामना कर के
उस पार की सूरज की देखने की हिम्मत करो तो सही... ।।
रास्ते तो हजारो है.. मगर
मंजिल को एक बार तुम चुनो तो सही..
सफर भी करना, मंजिल को गले भी लगाना तुम..
एक बार घर से निकलो तो सही ।।
नयी उड़ान भर रहा है ये दिल की परिंदा,
तुम मसरूफ बनने का मोका दो तो सही   वो
उड़ान भी भरेगा, खुले आसमान को अपनी जहां बनाएगा..

डियर डायरी

तुम्हारी और मेरी यारी कुछ निराली सी हे
ना मीठा ना खारी .
बस प्यारी सी हे ....(१)
कभी रो रो के तो
कभी खुसी और गम के आसुओं मे बरस पडती हू मे ..
पर तुम ना बड़े प्यार से उससे अपने पन्हो मे समेट लेते हो
साबासी न सही ...
मेरे कमियां भी तो नहीं गिनाते हो ... (२)

Dear डायरी. ....
लाखो उलझनों को ..
लाखो जज्बातों को रोज दफन करती हू यहां ......
और तुम भी बिना कुछ बोले बस मेरे साथ निभाते   चलते हो
दिलासा ना सही ....
मगर साथ होने के एहसास तो दिलाते हो ... (३)

Dear diary.. ..
तुम्हारी और मेरी यारी कुछ निराली सी हे ...
ना मीठा ना खरी ...
बस प्यारी सी है .... (४)
सुश्री आरती ...

Priyanka Sharma

Priyanka Sharma is 23 years old. She is students of bachelor of business administration at Nepal on butwal model college (Pokhara University). She lives in bhairahawa of Nepal. She is passionate about learning new things and she loves to click picture of nature whenever she travels through places of mountain & village. She loves to write quote & story.

The magic's of our thoughts I had a story to tell in my heart.
I also had my own story to tell.
I had dreams to tell.
I had also told my wish, but nothing happened as I thought.
Every difficulty that I sought made things worse over time.
Things that were very important then,
There was no meaning left in life.
Nothing is stable as time
Everything seems to be in the dark.
Not a single spark is gone.
Smile is gone nothing remains to be lost in despair

We're lucky we born in that generation where we used play in ground
Where we used wait 6 clock to play in ground with friends
Limitless talking in the roof late nights..
Our generation is different from today generation
I feel like to that we were in that generation
Which many youth can't feel why we used say?
Playing in ground, 7 stones game, cycling
Studying at morning, waiting cartoon time to come so we can see, completing homework to watch our favorite cartoon show...
I feel blessed that I enjoyed a lot in that generation of time

Ajay Kumar Jena

Ajay Kumar Jena is a Vocational Trainer and a great observer. He hails from Odisha and writing is his passion and this art is one of his greatest strength. Pen and paper are one of his closest companion. He loves to observe people's life and nature which helps him in writing.

Instagram - thisisajay28

"एक सवाल है आपसे पापा"

एक सवाल है आपसे पापा,
बिन बोले केसे मेरे दिल की बातें को जान लेते हो ।
ख्वाहिशें मेरी बिन कहे पूरे कर लेते हो,

खुद की शौक को मात देके...
मेरे हर एक शौक पूरे करते हो
मेरे हर ज़रूरत को खुद की ख्वाहिश बना लेते हो ।

एक सवाल है आपसे पापा, केसे ये सब कर लेते हो ?

मेरी हर गलती को,
सलहा देके नजर अंदाज कर देते हो ,
 हो जाए गलती मेरी,तो गुसे में डांट देते हो,
 फिर मन ही मन खुद को कोस लेते हो

एक सवाल है आपसे पापा, केसे ये सब कर लेते हो ?

खुद की जेब करके खाली,
मेरा जेब भर लेते हो,
शान से कहते भी हो,
के बताना और कुछ चाहिएं हो

एक सवाल है आपसे पापा, केसे ये सब कर लेते हो ?

देर रात आता हूं घर तो, आप मेरे लिए जगे रहते हो
मेरे सो जाने पर, कुछ गुन गुनाके मेरा माथा चूम लेते हो
बेहत करते हो प्यार, पर दिखावा नहीं करते हो

एक सवाल है आपसे पापा, केसे ये सब कर लेते हो ?

खुद की चिंता छोड़ के, मेरा खयाल रखा करते हो
मुझे कोई कमी ना हो, उसकी हिसाब करते रहते हो
जताते नहीं कुछ मगर, सब कुछ बयां हो जाता है
घर से दूर जब में जाता हूं, तो नमी आपकी आंखो में भी आता है ।

पत्थर सा दिल लेके, मुझे इस दरिया से पार करते हो...
बनके साया हमेशा मेरे साथ रहा करते हो..

आखिर एक सवाल है आपसे पापा, केसे ये सब कर लेते हो ?

ये सुनके पापा मुस्कुराके बोले....

वक़्त वक़्त का ये बात,
सब समझ में तुझे आयेगा
जिस दिन तुझे ये एहसास होगा,
उस दिन तू भी किसिका बाप होगा

Evinyne Miravite Novena

Evinyne miravite noveno
I am from Philippines
A reader and A writer
A beginner in the world of writing...
I use my pen to speak
What I see and what I feel about Through my quotations and poems ,..

To Let Go

Holding your hands
Hugging you tight
Kissing you deeply
Made me realize enough

I'm not the one you imagining
I'm not the one you wish for
To hug
To kiss
Even to hold your coldest hands
I'm asking myself ...
What I've done??
Looking at me that way
Your eyes answered me enough

 I'm just a shadow of his love that can never ever be real ...
It's not me ...
I'm not the one you love
My heart's catching
I can't hold you anymore...

You never ask me to let go of you
But your hearts pushing me away
Letting you go will make me
Feel relief..

I'm letting you go...

To Love Again

Don't think about what will happen
In the future , enjoy the moment
And let love decide ...
To the moment we are now
I'm so scared already for us,
Someone own you by fixed
But the one you love is me..
Yes,I did fallen already now
You teach me how to forgive myself
You teach me how to be happy again
You heal my dying heart
Who am I to be scared of...
I've cried enough and that's enough
Im willing to fight now for love...
I'm willing to accept what will happen ...
Because this time...

Shazia Jabeen

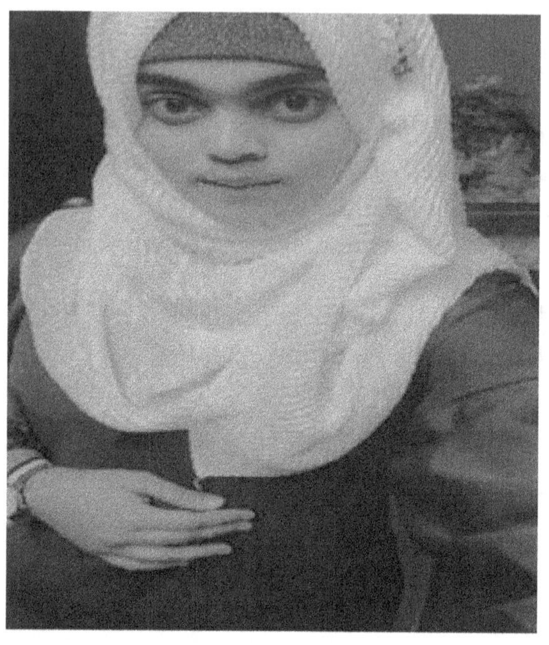

Name shazia jabeen
Anthologies : so Many
Studying: high school
Institute :Sri Chaitanya techno curriculum
Native place: tandur, vikarabad district, telengana

The Real Deal About Destiny

Destiny is your soul's dream for you. Your destiny can make you the happiest you can be. It is what you are best cut out for. It is what can give your life meaning, hope, joy and deep satisfaction.

You cannot screw up your destiny. It is impossible to miss out or mess up something that you are meant to experience. Hopefully this is reassuring to you. It may be especially reassuring if you are agonizing over a current decision or over-thinking a choice you already made.

The Five Elements of Reaching Your Destiny
Destiny is not a matter of chance. It is a matter of choice.
Know what you really, really, REALLY want.
Take action.
Get going and keep on going … no matter how you feel.
Avoid the destiny detours.
Break your big destiny into smaller, doable pieces.

It is not in the stars to hold our destiny but in ourselves." ...
"One love, one heart, one destiny." ...
"Letting go means to come to the realization that some people are a part of your history, but not a part of your destiny." ...
"There's nowhere you can be that isn't where you're meant to be..."

Mahima Lodhi

name mahima lodhi 10th class student from bhopal age 16 year continue study in shramodaya vidyalaya bhopal also self depend

If you can dreams and not make dreams your mistake
If you can think and not make thoughts your aIm
If you can meet Truimph and Diaster and treet those two
impostors just the same

If you can bear to hear the truth you ve spoken
Twisted by knaves to make a trap for fools
Or watch the things you gave your life to broken
And stop and build em up with worn out tools

Shaheen Shah

Myself Shaheen shah from bangalore.
Love to express my thoughts,so started writing.

together was only meant in imagination for them but it was never written in their destiny to be one.
An story of two souls,who were strangers to eachother.
He was an introvert,she was an extrovert both were opposite to eachother but something was interesting in their life which made them fall for eachother.
Randomly she texted him "hii" on instagarm and in seconds he replied back as "don't text me or else I will block you".
She texted him "ooh,Mr.whoever you are don't act much,just talk to me because I'm feeling bored in which he said "ooh,girl go away or else"...
This conversation was something interesting which made him to reply her back as soon as possible.
Later ..numbers were changed,chatting till 3am,videocalls, finally planned to meet eachother etc..
Met eachother, promised to be always stay but he said I'm no more gonna continue this relationship as society always sees caste ,religion and definitely they will no more .

Keerthana

Keerthana hails from Chennai,Tamil Nadu
A girl of sixteen running towards her dream,
Full of Hope, finding her happiness in the smallest things.
 She's a blend of emotions trying to express it through her writings.
She loves to be a hodophile and explore the world. She adds up with music which lights the world.
Her main goal is to motivate people around her and spread positivity with smiles forever.
She has accomplished great goals in sports, oraetorical competitions and waiting for many more to attain the destiny
You can find her writings relatable @quotes_by_girly_writer

Bealive In You

Everyday is a new beginning. Wakeup with a ray of positivity that you could achieve something great and make the day favourable to you. Impossible is nothing, just excuses meant for lazy people. Excuses and reasons are common and only loosers keep asking and searching. Consistency is the key to success. Problems are not too big;we are too small to handle them. There are people whose life is greatest problem and still they survive . Problems should brings changes in us. They break us ,heal us,damage our soul forever. But finally we become better stronger and powerful. The best lessons are taught with painful feelings and with pain.Make yourself engaged. Make yourself as a role model and make others to choose you as a role model. Never follow other's path. Create your own path and make it define. Make sure that consistency in your hardest tasks even in bad times,you should do it which will bring up colorful results and helps to taste the sweetest destination called success. Procasination leads to failure. It puts our energy down and makes our mind dumb.Sometimes it's now or never.

Optimism: The Peak of Life

Life is all about facing ups & Downs in every situation , but every time when you fall down, You learn something new and you will get an unforgettable experience!!. After gaining all the experiences you'll be tired of trying. But if you remain stubborn not to give up and get back up you ll succeed with the your hardwork and efforts. You will feel like flying in the sky with loads of enjoyment , likely to be the happiest person in the world. That's why I tell life is beautiful. Whenever you are sad just think about someone who has no shelter , no food , no clothing. When compared, we are blessed. We are the happiest person in the world as God has selected and provided us with the gifted abilities. We are gifted as we are able to enjoy and feel all the little things happening around which makes our life beautiful. After rain when you find the rainbow you just admire the beauty of it along with it's cloudy climate. In the early morning when the rooster cocks you admire the minute hidden beautiful things which gives you the feeling that you are gifted!!

Kiran Maurya

Kiran Mourya is 20 year old Statistics student at Central university of Rajasthan in Ajmer . She is from Jaipur city of Rajasthan . She is not a professional writer but try to do something with pen. She have a 3 year experience in your quote.

Her pen name is mysterious writer.

Insta_id:- kiranmourya6799

#सफ़र अधूरा मत छोड़ो

सफर अधूरा मत छोड़ो,
हार मिले कोई बात नहीं ,
फिर पूरी शक्ति से प्रहार करो ,
जीत मिलेगी इक दिन तुझको,
यही सोचकर बारम बार प्रयास करो,
अगर छोड़ोगे सफर अधूरा तो,
तुम जीत अधूरी ही पाओगे ,
फिर ना कहना विफल हो गए ,
किये प्रयत्न भी व्यस्त हो गए,
फिर डुबो कर खुद को हार में ,
तुम अंधकार से गिरा पाओगे ,
फिर ना होगा उजाला जीवन में ,
तुम मृत्य खुद को इस अंधकार में पाओगे ,
इसीलिए कहती हूं सफर अधूरा मत छोड़ो,
किए प्रयत्न पर पानी मत फेरो...!!

#अभी तुझ से करना मेरा इश्क बाकी है

क्या हुआ जो तुम चले गए यूं बीच सफर में छोड़ कर,
अभी मेरे हिस्से का साथ निभाना बाकी है,
अभी तुझसे करना मेरा इश्क बाकी है,

हां ! तुमने तो निभा ली आपने हिस्से की नफ़रत,
पर अभी मेरे हिस्से का प्यार निभाना बाकी है ,
अभी तुझ से करना मेरा इश्क बाकी है ,

चले गये तुम तो हमें अपनी यादों से मिटा कर
पर अभी तुझे मेरी यादों में आना बाकी है ,
अभी तुझ से करना मेरा इश्क बाकी है,

हां! भूल तो जाओगे तुम हमें एक अरसे के बाद ,
पर अभी तुझेइक अरसे तक याद करना बाकी हैं,
अभी तुझसे करना मेरा इश्क बाकी है ।।

Simran Rajpal

Simran Rajpal Is A 18 Year Old Medical Student At RLT College Of Akola.She Is From Akola City Of Maharashtra. She is not a writer but loves to be expressive and beautifully trace her emotions into her quotes.

1. Expecting wrong things from wrong people,.
is the biggest mistake I made...
I expected loyalty from a person
Who can't even give me honesty....

2. Forget the things that made you sad,
And remember those that made you glad.
Forget the past events that passed away,
And remember the opportunities that are yet to come every
day.

3. People say what you were in your past,
Is being reflected in your future....
But I do wonder..., really is it so?
inner voice answered....,
No it is not so.
Life is just like a game where ,
You can't predict the result till the last ball....
life is just an unpredictable journey.

4. It's not all what you say....
But what you do that really matters
After all.....
Action is more powerful than words.

SP Vidya

Myself sp vidya 21 yrs old Pursuing final year bsc graduation and my ambition is to serve the country my thoughts
 My insta id sp_vidya

Bin Bulaye Mehman

Kya corona hum ko quarantine ha
Abb aur hamara zindagi nahi basti
Shayad tujame bhi
ek choti se dil basti
Maan mai ek hi sawal
Tumne aake uthna acha bhi kya kiya
Na jaane tumara na jaane ka
Hamnae uthna bura bhi kya kiya
Continued
Thera entry marne ke baad
Chal amir log bajate
Garib log mar jaate
Hum middle class wale kare bhi tho kya kare Mana ki
tumara aane ke baad
Sambandhi ki sanskriti badi
Srishti ka acha sangharsh huva
Acha chal tumare aane ka aamantran
Humnae nahi diya ,bharat ki naam
"Atithi Devo Bhava"se hi jana jata hai
Ab waqt hai tumhara vidhayi ka
Bas dua hai tumhara dubara na aane ka

Shreeja Sathish

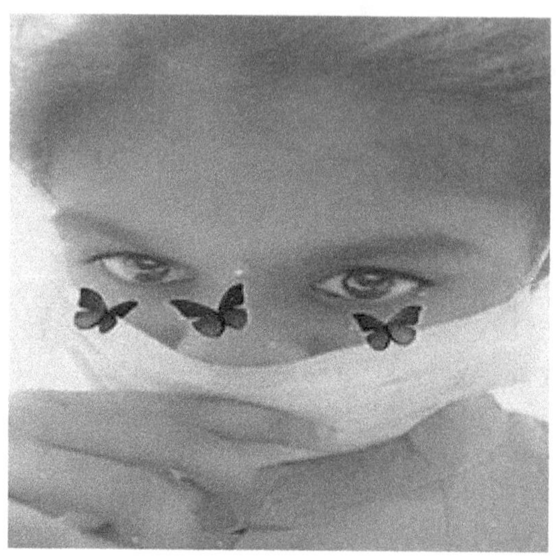

Shreeja Sathish is 11 year old. Student of sri Chaitanya school. Chennai city of tamilnadu. She likes to show her talent through pen

Old Man And The Little Girl

One day the little girl asked her grandma for some potatoes and the old man was a famer.The old man answer to the little girl that i am a famer i will farm the potatoes and i will give you .the little was so happy and the old man stared farming. Days past and the little girl asked for potatoes and it stared raining the old man said to her don't cry little girl i will bring you the potatoes now. And the old man prayed to the god to stop the rain and suddenly the rain stopped and the old man got some potatoes from is farm and the little girl was so happy.The old man asked why you asked me potatoes. The little girl said i love to cook potatoes and i love to eat them grandma and the old man said ok and for me also some potatoes

Jyoti Mourya

Jyoti mourya is 20 year old M.Sc (statistics) student at CENTRAL UNIVERSITY OF RAJASTHAN.
She is from jaipur, Rajasthan. She loves to write quotes and story .She wants do something for society through her pen.

1) सब सही हैं
जब ये ना पता हो गलत क्या है तब कह देना
सब सही है ।
जब यह ना पता हो कि गलत को सही कैसे करना है , तब कह देना
सब सही है ।।
जब दर्द गहरा हो और आंखों से आंसू छलंकर चेहरे पर मुस्कुराहट
लिए हो , तब कह देना सब सही है ।।
जब टूट कर बिखर जाओ और इन मोतियों को समेटकर फिर से
इनकी माला बनाने वाला कोई ना हो , तब कह देना सब सही है ।।
जब परछाई साथ छोड़ कर जाते हुए उंगली दूसरों की पकड़ कर
मुस्कुराने लगे , तब कह देना सब सही है ।। जब अपना बंधन किसी
की खुशी बन जाए , तब कह देना सब सही है ।। सब सही हैं

2) आदत नही है चाय का प्याला हर रोज पीने की , बस तलब हैं इन
आंखों को एक शख्स को हर रोज देखने की .. !!

3) निहत्थे ही चलेंगे दुश्मनों की बजाने ए दोस्त ... हथियार छोड़ , बस
कलम ले आना ... !!

4) ये खेल,ये किताबे,ये शेर-ओ-शायरियां ये जिंदगी एक जंग है , जारी
थी..जारी है जारी रहेगी जब तक ये सांसे जिंदगी- ए- खुदा ने लिखी हैं
...!!

5) जिंदगी की धूप में तपते एक मजदूर की अनकही दास्तां जिंदगी की
कड़कती धूप में , मजदूरी की आस में निकल गए कुछ लोग सवेरे ही
अपने घरों से , मैंने सुना है घर चलाने निकले हैं ।। कल रात एक रोटी
चार हिस्सों में बंटी थी मैंने सुना है कल दो मुसाफिर उन्हीं के घर रुके
थे ।। निकल गए फटे हाल बाजार में , मजदूरी की आस में हाथों में दो
रोटी लिए , मैंने सुना है अपने बच्चों की मुस्कान खरीदने निकले हैं ।।

Ayushi Mishra

Ayushi mishra
Age :15 years, study in 11 class,

झलो रानी इधर आ तो...!! ये सेंटेंस मानो उसके लिए उसकी पहचान बन गया है 12 साल की राधिका जिसे ये तो पता था कि उसकी ड्रेस फटी है पर मां उसे नई ड्रेस क्यों नहीं दिला रही इसका जवाब वह जानते हुए भी अनजान रहना चाहती थी। Class का हर एक बच्चा उस झल्लो रानी ही कहता अब वो अपना दर्द सुनाती भी तो किसे फटी ड्रेस आज तक किसे ही भाई है सो उसके भी जानने वालों को ना भाती। रोज सब नए नए तरीके बनाते उसे परेशान करने के लिए उसे हर बात का बुरा लगता पर चुप हो अपनी मां की तस्वीर देख लेती। आज दीवाली थी झललो रानी घर के बाहर दिए जला रही थी उसका पूरा घर चमचमा रहा था छोटा भाई से लेकर भाई की गुड़िया तक बस जो चमक नहीं रहा था तो वो थी झालो रानी सब दंग थे। अगली सुबह पूरी class झाल्लो रानी का इंतेज़ार कर रही थी पर पहला प्रियोड निकाल गया पर उसका कोई पता नहीं चला।   की तभी झलों रानी class में दाखिल हुई उसके पूरे शरीर पर दाग थे, थोड़ी थोड़ी सूजन भी शरीर में शरीक थी। उसने थोड़ी उदास शब्दो में कहा मैम जी मेरा नाम काट दीजिए बस इतना ही कहते वो रोने लगी मैम ने पूछा तो बस यू हू छोड़ रही हूं जवाब दे कर बाहर चली गई सभी बच्चे इधर उधर की बाते मन में ला रहे थे कि तभी एक आवाज आई अरे बस भी करो राधिका के बारे में एशियाई वैसा बोलना.! मै बताती है क्या हुआ है... राधिका की मम्मी उसकी पढ़ाई छुड़वा रही है। सब ने उस शक्स से पूछा कि "पर क्यों अरे भाई झालों को तो पढ़ाई क बोहोत शोक था" तभी शकस ने जवाब दिया अरे वो उसकी अपनी नहीं सौतेली मम्मी है ना

Madhvi Jha

Madhvi jha is 18 years old b.sc student.i am from bihar

Manjil ki chah ne hamein musafir bana diya Muskilon ne ek dafa fir mera rasta bana diya.

53

Shor ki Chahat rakhne wale logaksar khamoshiyon me palte h

Soniya Varghese

Soniya Varghese is a degree student and an emerging writer.She is specialising her degree in English teaching.She is going to be a co-author in the upcoming anthology named "The Ghost Of Loneliness",and is aiming to do more.

Pre- Destined Relationship

Pre-destined relationship,it means that two people might been fated to meet,in the end they were not destined to remain together.Whenever someone falls in love their world seems to be bound with their loved ones.Same goes for me too.Seven years ago I was an ordinary girl who goes to school and returns home after having fun with friends.One day a boy told me that he loves me.I couldn't say anything but we were destined to meet.I fell for him with passing time.

Our relationship had no problems,it was as sweet as honey.But because of some circumstances we couldn't be together for two years.We completely lost touch.But I believed in destiny.I knew that we'll meet someday and we did.We were destined to be together and we again started our relationship from where it stopped.But this timebour relationship had no boundaries.Because of our age and our feelings there was no restricted boundaries.We were falling for each other every time we met.

It was all going perfectly alright.We had plenty of time to meet each other.We did all that we couldn't do.We were like free birds.No one was there for restricting is.We were loving each other like it was going to be the end of world.We had fights but every fight ended up in loving each other more and more.

But again we had to face problems.This time our families didn't wanted us to be together.We were facing challenges each and every time.Whenever we were happy struggles came up like hills.But this time we proved to them that we won't leave each other whatever we may have to face.If we were destined to be together we will be.Finally,they had to agree and hence we are leading a peaceful life.

Believe in destiny it'll take you to your pre-destined destination.

Reetika Singh

Reetika Singh. Born in Bihar. She is 19 and has acheived multiple recognitions apart from poetry. She is an international sports champion in Karate and has completed her diploma in Shotokan Karate 1st Dan. Besides all this she is a virtual artist. She has a versatile nature.

Do you ever wake up in the middle of the night and just think
about where you thought you were gonna be at this point in
life?
I said no to a lot of things the world has told me
I'm supposed to say yes to.
I lost a lot of things I really thought I needed.
You always end up where you are supposed to be.
Even if it hurts a lot getting there.
IT'S ALWAYS WORTH IT.
we are all buckets,
waiting to be filled.
our insides are hollowed and filtered,
left empty and all alone.
This ravenous gaping hole within us creates the strong desire
to be fulfilled.
we sustain our hungry ears with gossip, thin and
unsatisfactory.
We reveal our eyes to the never-ending platforms of social
media that seemingly entertain us where we don't have to
think at all.
Our noses smell the most pungent of crudeness,
putting others down to distract us from how low we feel
ourselves.
Our mouths, our lips, our tongues, taste the palate of lies
strung to form sentences that coil within us.
Our hands search the crevices of each other , thinking that
through touch we will be able to feel something more than
this black hole that annihilates us.
It gives us the illusion that we are full and satisfied.
When really, we are all starving corpses, on the edge of
death, living a life that isn't ours.
A life that is formulated off a foundation of lies and sorrow.
A LIFE THAT WE CAN NO LONGER LIVE

Ruchika Bansal

Myself Ruchika bansal from New delhi....
Working in delhi government school as teacher.....nd I write
because it gives me satisfaction

मै हूं कौन

जब पूछा गया मुझसे
तुम हो कौन
सोच मेरी रुक गई
हो गया मै मौन
क्या मै हूं पांच फिट का शरीर
या इसके अंदर समाया ज़मीर
या अंतरात्मा हैं मेरी तस्वीर
या मै हूं ख़ुद के हाथों की लकीर
या बस हूं इस मन की जागीर
या हूं असीम ख्वाहिशों का वज़ीर
हूं कोई राजा या एक फ़कीर
क्या मै हूं अपने लक्ष्य के लिए गंभीर
क्या मै हूं निराकार में समाने को अधीर
विचार नहीं ये गौण
आखिर मै हूं कौन

दृश्य मौत का

निगाहों में छुपाकर
दिलों में बसाकर
यत्न थे कर रहें
उसे भुलाने को
जिन आंखों में था खटकता
वे भी थे तैयार अब
प्यार लुटाने को
कुछ आतुर थे
शरीर से उसके
कीमती चीज़ें उतारने को
तो कुछ थे बेचैन
लेकर जायदाद के
बंटवारे को
अब बस थी ज़रूरत
चार लोगों की
उठाने को
जिनके दिलों में थी

Rinkal N. Dhokiya

I am Rinkal Dhokiya, age - 25, Live in Mumbai Bandra, I am Advocate by profession, I started writing last year October 2020 by then I have written 3 anthologies successfully & look forward for more to it, I love to inspire & motivate people for their betterment

Love Twice After Self Love

a four letter word which has a deep meaning in life of every individual but what does it actually mean to one. It is as abstract as it sounds, in today's world it is so hard to define a true love and a fake love but actually loves has no types, it is we who give it a sub names. We people have confused its meaning but in actual love all does is heal you, heal your deepest wounds, it is very wrong to say atleast in my opinion that "Love hurts", no it does not hurt, what hurts you is your own expectations. Love has always been pure in its own form.Love has many forms love comes to you in many ways such as family, friend, desires, job, partner and so on but it all starts from "ME"when first you love yourself when you accept yourself to the fullest when you love yourself so much that no one can dare enter your vicinity to hurt you and that's how Love heals you. But we instead finding love in ourselves we go out to find it and mess up everything and blame that love hurts.So my dear friend if your cup is empty what will you pour in others cup,

Failure

A word which is not pleasing to our ears and our hearts, a word which we fail to concede in our life. We fear failure so much that we are in constant struggle with it in our day to day life, but what we need to understand here today is that though failure is not something we want to see in our life but it is as necessary as success, failure is harsh but it is one of the best educator in one's life. It plays a very important role in our life.For an instance just imagine you being successful without failing in your life for single time, how do you see your success ? isn't it raw? Success won't teach what failure can. Failure gives your experience, knowledge, it makes you resilient to withstand quickly from difficult conditions, it takes you towards your growth, it also helps you bring value to the table. When you are successful what more speaks is what you have learnt throughout your life and that comes when you have gained experience through your hardships and your failures.So my dear friend do not fear failure instead overcome your fears by .

Samyuktha Sathish

Samyuktha sathish is 13 year old. Student of sri chaitanya school. She is from chennai city of Tamilnadu. She wants to achieve something big and make her parents proud.

The Deer And The Beauty

In a big forest there lived a deer with beautiful horns. It felt thirsty. There was a pond nearby. While drinking water it saw it's reflection in it and said itself by seeing it's beautiful horns "wow what a beautiful horns I have. I am really proud of it "At the same time it saw it's legs and said "yuck what a ugly leg I have, and am really ashamed of it ".suddenly it noticed a sound like some one coming towards it. It turned it's head around and saw a hunter coming towards it with a big gun. It started running into the forest and hidden behind the bushes. It listened to the Hunter's words.

"Ohh I missed a beautiful horns nooo "he shouted. The deer found that he has come to take it's horns by killing it and it thanked to it's leg "Ohh leg I am really sorry, now I am really proud of you, you saved my life, thank you so much "And realised appearance doesn't matter, and beauty is sometimes harmful. So what ever we have is God's gift. Be happy with what you have.

Shama Kamra

Shama Kamra is a homemaker and a beautiful woman who can write her feelings, emotions and her observations about life, love and many other things. She has a great sense of music in her life and she believes that everything can be okay if you just believe.

1. एक दिन में कोई भी "गुलज़ार" नहीं बनता,,,
मेहनत लगती है तब जाकर गुलफाम बना करते हैं,
रोज नया फूल खिलता है बगिया में,
पर हर फूल को महकने का मुक़द्दर नहीं मिलता, कौन चढेगा श्री
हरि चरणों में,
कौन अर्थी पर,
कौन बनेगा हिस्सा किसी रुपसी के श्रंगार का , सब तय हो चुका
पहले से ही, इस तरह कब कौन मिलेगा बिगडेगा पहले ही तय
किया वक्त होता है,जिंदगी के रंग मंच पर हर कोई निभा रहा
बखूबी किरदार अपना, जो समझ गया डोर किसी के हाथ में है वो
हो गया राजी, जो कर गया नासमझी वो फंस के रह गया बस
शिकवे शिकायतों में ही !!

2. तुने वक्त जो तय करके दिया मुझे सुनने का,,,
मेरी आधी उलझनों को सहारा मिल जाता है सुलझने का,,,

3. रोज देखती हूँ जब तुझे मशरुफ काम में,,,,
 मेरी रगों में इक खुशी की लहर उमडती है,
कामयाबी उसकी तो असर रखती है जरुर जी जिस शख्स की छाप
दिल की गहराईयों में छपी होती है !

4. दिल से शुक्रिया सभी का जिन्होंने अपनी दुआओं के काबिल समझा हमें,,,,,
ये दिल की दीवारें ईश्वर ने इतनी कोमल इसलिए बनाई है कि प्यार की

 हल्की सी आहट भी झट सुनाई दे जाये, ये प्यार ही है जो बड़ी बड़ी मुश्किलों में मज़बूत बनाता है, कौन कितना नजदीक है या दूर मायने नहीं रखता बस प्यारी सी मुस्कान के साथ दिल में घर कर लेता है !!

5. काश समझ पाते आप जरूरी क्या है ,,,
तो चेहरे पर आज भी नूर बरकरार होता

6. तुझे सोचने भर से ही जब बेचैनीयो को राहत मिल जाती है , तो जरूर कुछ ऐसा खास
है ना तुझमें!

Pooja Gautam

इन्होंने इतिहास विषय में सन्नातकोत्तर की शिक्षा प्राप्त की है। यह ज़्यादातर स्त्रियों के उत्थान के विषय में लिखना पसंद करती है। इनके लेखन के केंद्र बिंदु समाज के लोग ही है, जिनसे यह अपने लेखन से उभारने की कोशिश करती है। इन्होंने शायरी, निबंध, लेख, कविताएं आदि कई प्रतियोगिताओं में भाग लिया है, जिनके लिए इन्हें सम्मानित भी किया गया है। इनका मानना है कि कर्म ही प्रधान है, इसलिए हर इन्सान को पुरुषार्थ करना चाहिए।

मार्मिक स्पर्श चित्रण

जहन्नुम की गलियां शायद उस बंद कमरे की चुभन से बेहतर थी जहां खुद को चार दिवारी के बीच छुपाए, हमने सालों गुज़ार दिए आने और जाने का रास्ता सिर्फ एक था, जहां से धुंधली सी किरण
मुझे एक ओट से देख लेती थी सामने बैठी मेरी नज़र सामने घड़ी की सुइयों पर होती थी, जो रुक रुक चलती थी, सलवटों सा एक बिछोना मेरी तबाही का राज़दार था इसलिए साथ ही रहता था.. ज़मीं की कुछ धूल मेरी किताबों पर भी लगी थी, शायद कहना चाहती हो, मैं पुरानी हो गई हूं ज़रूरत इतनी किसी की मेरी थी नहीं, बस कुछ पन्ने साथ रखती थी, मेरी गवाही ही समझ लीजिए पर बात तो ये थी कि मैं शव भांति थी, जिसके पीछे प्रश्नवाचक चिन्ह लगा जो खुद से भी अनभिज्ञ थी।

सफ़र

ज़िन्दगी के सफ़र में क्या पाया मैंने, क्या खो दिया, मायने इस बात के इतने नहीं थे, बस कुछ दो कदम चलने की बात थी, उन पथरीली सड़कों के साथ जहां वो रोज़ आघात सहती थी। वो दर्द.. वो एहसास.. इतना ही जानना था मुझे, रास्तों की लंबाई नहीं नापनी थी.. बस एक औरत का रिश्ता जोड़ना था.. उस ज़िन्दगी के साथ,जो शुरू से अंत तक.. वो लहूलुहान पैरों को खींचते हुए.. अब तक जिंदा है..एक लड़की से इस बुढ़ापे तक के सफ़र.. में कितने पहाड़, पगडंडियां ,नदी, नाले बीच राह देखे.. सब व्यस्त महसूस हो रही थी,जैसे देख कर भी..अनदेखा किया सब ने,क्या मैं सच में दिखती नहीं थी? मैंने तो खुद को सालों से नहीं देखा..जाने झुर्रियों की तब्दीली.. और इन केशों की रंगत.. मेरे वक़्त की वो बातें बता रही थी,जो गुज़रे सफ़र मैं बहुत पीछे छोड़ आई थी।बीच राह मुझे ऐसे भी मिले, जिनकी आंखे मेरे चेहरे पर थी,शायद कोई कमज़ोरी मेरी, उन्हें दिखने लगी थी पर शुक्रगुज़ार उनके कुछ पल ही सही, किसी ने हमारी पहचान तो की, जो इन रास्तों में बता गए, कि मैं भी उन दो आंखों के बीच शामिल थी.जहां कुछ पल मुरझाई चमड़ी को देखा जाता है। वास्तविकता ये है, कि इस सफ़र में सुकून की एहमियत कुछ रह जाती नहीं क्यूंकि शोर तो लोगों का साथ-साथ चल ही रहा था। इस अधूरे सफ़र में मैं आज तक चल ही रही थी क्यूंकि इस सफ़र का अंतिम पड़ाव कुछ था ही नहीं।

Shemila

Shemila Sheikh
BSC computer science student
From Maharashtra
To express my feelings I started writing..

Shemi_0608Black heart girl°

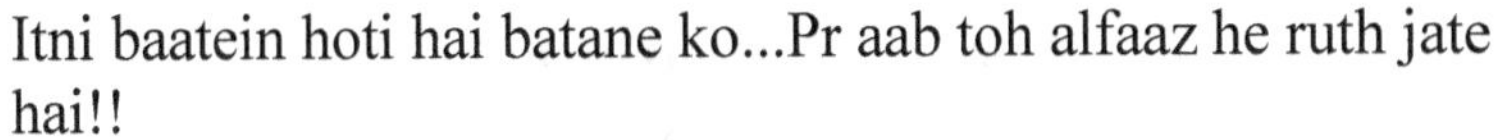

Itni baatein hoti hai batane ko...Pr aab toh alfaaz he ruth jate hai!!

73

Mohabbat krni he hai toh rooh se karo...Jism ki chahat toh har koi rkhta hai..

Hema Kirthiga J

She is Hema Kirthiga J, and her pen name is sparkle. She is professionally a psychologist and passionately a writer. She heals others but writing heals her. She is writer, reader, orator and a believer. She is from Chennai. She lives by the principal of inspire and be inspired. She writes her heart and soul and she deeply believes that the depth of her heart and the nib of her pen are soulfully connected. Writing is an art and she is a proud artist. She loves what she does and loves what she writes. You can reach her at
Instagram-
@the_pen_queen
Email- inker.sparkle@gmail.comYourquote – JKM

What Is My Destiny?

Is it death?
No i shall live,
Till i achieve my dream.

Is it love?
Sometimes yes,
But i want to live forever,
with the person i love.

Is it health?
With good health,
I can conquer everything,
but i want far more than that.

Is it friends,
They are the good soul,
But i want to reach my destiny with them.

Is it dreams?
They are not,
Because i want to achieve my dream,
Live well and slap on those who betrayed me.

Then what is your destiny?
I don't know,
I am just walking towards destiny,
Its an endless path.

Harshita (Manu)

Harshita(Manu) is a 13 year old school students writing for more than 7 years. Born in Bokaro Steel City, Jharkhand. Currently has no proper writing record. Writting isn't just her habit, it's her own way.

Hate, evoL
I am all alone
So don't dare say that
My friendship is a great one
I inherit a fake smile to hide my true tears
So don't you even think that
I smile quite happily
I have known the worst fake love
But I never was able to know
The loveliest true love
I have always been exposed to
I am always been exposed to
The darkest side of the world
But I was never able to say
I know the brightest side of the world
I know the side that is only filled with love and happiness
I truly love myself
But it's not possible because.
I literally hate myself
(Read bottom up)

It's you
I was dying
Because I was living for you
I hid my tears
For you to smile
I spoiled my life
For making your life
I lived alone
For you to get a good company
I did hurt me
For you to be safe
I never told you my love
For you to get your love
I really died
For you to live a happy and beautiful life.

Krish Balani

KRISH BALANI is 16 year old class XI student at SN College Akola. He is from Akola city of Maharashtra. He is a true writer and writing is his passion. He hopes to help fight social evils with his pen.

1. Life is very beautiful but you have to keep your mobile aside and give time.

2. People live for their parents but I owe my whole life to my parents.

3. 2020 not only made us sit home instead it taught us to explore life without moving out of the house and also gave us a very great experience of real and fake people.

4. Social distancing is to be implemented physically but some people are so devotional to it that they have even implemented it among minds and hearts too.

5. If a smile can make our selfie pretty so why shouldn't we keep a smile on our face forever to make our whole life pretty.

6. Clothes never get old fashioned just people change their way of observing the world.

7. Elders are never a bane for the world instead they are a treasure of experience for the next generations.

8. Winners never just dream to be successful, they leave their comfort zone and make their dream come true to sleep peacefully.

Sukanya Gunja

Dr Sukanya gunja hails from the town m Andhra Pradesh. She was born on 10th June 1996. She was born in a christian family. Right from her early childhood her ambition was to become a doctor. She went on to do her bachelor's in veterinary medicine. She is an introvert. She is not a professional writer but want to share her feelings through her writings.... She likes to motivate others and bring them out of their pain and sadness....

Be like a salt....
Add taste to everyone's life those who enter yours life....
Not less not much...but..perfect...
If coal can turn into diamond...and sand into pearls...then
definitely your love will turn stone hearted people to soft...
If one drop of poison can kill a person....just one drop of love
can change a person....
Heartbreak... is going to teach you a lesson not to break it
again and again....
Stop crying...
Keep trying...
Life is neither a bed of roses nor a road of thorns...
It's like a rose garden having both beautiful roses and
thorns....
Many of us struggle overcome our past...
It could be our past habits that have destroyed our health...
Or it could be our past relationships that have crushed us and
caused so much hurt...

Or it could be our actions that have costed our peace....
Let go of the past.....start your new life....
I wish my life would be like a Korean drama...
Korean dramas will always have a happy ending even if it
was sad at starting...But...I don't know how my life would
be...I'm having a sad life...
Yes...we know that it is a drama but not real that's why there
is always a happy ending. Our life is not a drama to have a
happy ending...
In drama all characters are fake...in our lives also the people
who entered into our life are also fake....
To heal a wound....It requires regular cleaning and dressing...
Likewise to heal a wound in your heart you just have to clean
those past life and dressed with new memories...

Shradha Gindlani

Shradha Gindlani is from a small town with big dreams taking hold of her heart and brain, day and night. With a vision of community to serve those in need of education and literacy she aspires high. She writes poetries and prose mainly . She is kind hearted and helping personality indeed.

I Wish Time Has.....

I wish time had better timing for you and me,
Enraged and caged, fret and fever of life
Distancing the bonds of God and mine
Making us a slave treading unimaginative strives.
Destiny is not lending us relieved sighs
I wish time had better timing for God and I

Pramila Rawat

Pramila Rawat is a teacher and lives in Dehradun. She is a resident of Uttarakhand. She has been interested in writing since her school days. Her creations are inspired by the events and characters around her. She is a realistic writer.

कभी ख़्याल मेरा आया?

सुनो,कभी ख़्याल मेरा आया था,क्या कभी मेरी याद आई,
यहां की तपिश वहां गई तो होगी,उसने कुछ तो मजबूर किया
होगा,हम इतने बुरे भी न थे,कि हम याद ही न आएं, जब पहाड़ो से
ठंडी हवा छू जाती होगी और
सर्दियों की गुनगुनी धूप सुहावनी लगती होगी,
जब कभी आंख तुम्हारी नम हुई होगी,और हम आँसू बन कर गाल
तक पहुँचे होंगे,जब उन आँसुओ के खारापन का स्वाद चखा
होगा,तब तो याद आये होंगे,
जब किसी अपने ने डाँट दिया होगाऔर जब बहुत परेशान हो जाती
होंगी,तब याद आये होंगे,
जब- जब इस दिल से टीस निकली होगी,
तब वो दिल कुछ भारी तो हुआ होगा,तब याद किया होगा,जब
किसी मंदिर की चौखट में मेरा माथा ,
तुम्हारी याद में झुका होगा,तब तो याद आयी होगी,
जब जब तुम्हारी सलामती के लिए दुआ मांगी होगी,
तब तो जरूर तुम तक पहुँची होगी,
जब कभी हमको ठोकर लगी होगी और जुबाँ से तुम्हारा नाम
निकला होगा,तब तो तुमने सुना होगा ,तब मुझे जरूर याद किया
होगा ना,एक बार तो ख्याल आया होगा

यूँ तो कई बार ख्याल तुम्हारा आया था,

जब -जब दुखों का समन्दर लहराया था,

जब दर्द भरी रातों ने जगाया था,

तब टूटती हिम्मत को हमने खुद ढाँढस बँधाया था,

तो आकर तुमने ही तो पीठ को थपथपाया था,

वैसे तो कई बार ख्याल तुम्हारा आया था,

जब पहली बार कोई रिश्ता आया था,

तो भरी महफ़िल में भी खुद को बहुत तन्हा पाया था,

माँ के आँसू, फिक्र और लोक रीत के बीच,

जब जीवन की संभावनाओं को खोजा था,

तो अजनबी राहों और अनजाने लोगों में,

बस तुम्हे ही तो तलाशा था,

बहुत बातें थी दिल में, दर्द भी पुराना था,

और दुःखों ने तो जैसे कब्ज़ा जमाया था,

कोई होता जिस से लिपट कर सारे दुःख कह सकते,

पर कोई सीना न मिला,न कोई काँधा,न हाथ किसी ने बढ़ाया था,

उस वक़्त,सिर्फ ख़्याल तुम्हारा आया था,

फिर एक चेतना जागी और जीवन का रुख़ मोड़ लिया,

अपने ही अंक में, अपने अंश से,जीवन को जोड़ लिया,

वो चेतना का सूर्य तुमने ही तो जगाया था,

हाँ, बहुत याद आयी तुम्हारी,

सिर्फ ख़्याल तुम्हारा आया था,

Akanksha Gupta

आकांक्षा गुप्ता, महादेवी वर्मा जी की जन्मस्थली फ़र्रूख़ाबाद (उ.प्र.) की रहने वाली हैं । वह एक राधा कृष्णा भक्त और कृष्ण पर लिखने वाली और उभयमुखी व्यक्तित्व की कवयित्री हैं । उन्होंने बीएड किया हुआ है उनका निजी शिक्षा संस्थान है । लोगों को शिक्षित करना उनका शौक है । उनका मानना है कि कलम में बहुत बड़ी ताकत होती है जो काम तलवार नहीं कर सकती है वो काम एक कलम कर सकती है इसलिए वो अपनी कलम के द्वारा हर मुद्दे पर अपने विचार प्रकट कर लोगों को जागरूक करती हैं।उनको इंस्टाग्राम पे फॉलो कर सकते हैं @devnagri_poetry

akan7454ag@gmail.com पर संपर्क करें

ये मुरली जान ले लेगी बनी सौतन हमारी है ।
नहीं इस से निकट कोई यही मोहन को प्यारी है ।
सखी चलो छोड़ दें ब्रज हम चलो जमुना में बह जाएं,
रहेगी मुरली ही ब्रज में जरूरत क्या हमारी है ?
धरी अधरों पे मोहन के बहुत इठलाती है खुद पर,
हमें नीचा दिखती है बनी दुनिया से न्यारी है ।
कान्हा आज सच कह दो अधिक तुम्हें कौन प्यारा है,
साथ वेणु के रहना है या हम सखियों से यारी है ।
ये मुरली जान...
छेड़ो जब तान वंशी की तो सबकुछ भूल जाते हो,
मुरलिया त्याग दो मोहन कसम तुमको हमारी है।
ये मुरली जान ..
हमारे घर का सब माखन तुम्हें दे देंगे हम कान्हा,
तुम ये मुरली हमें दे दो,जरूरत हमको भारी है।
ये मुरली जान..

Kiran

I'm kiran 24 years old   studying in rofel MBA
vapi
Stay in valsad gujrat 396001
I always take a participate in international essay writing
competition shri ramchandr heartfullness
And i wanna become a great writer

Suicide

Bhagwaan ne khubsurat zindagi se nvaza hai ise ji bhar k jeeye, marna to hai 1 din fir suicide ka pap na kijiye. Zindagi h dard, tklif to degi hi aj jitna diya h kl uska dugna degi iska mtlb ye nhi ki hm yesa kadam utha le agar sb marne lge to zindagi jeena kese h vo sikhega kon.

aksar hm zindagi se lad nhi pate, muskilo ka samna nhi kr pate, rejection, failure, financial problems ye sb face nhi kr pate. Kbhi yesa hota h ki hme family ka support bhi nhi milta to hm preshan ho jate h, kya kre kya na kre soch hi nhi pate, iska mtlb ye to nhi ki zindagi buri ! hm bas kosis hi nhi krna chahte. Darte h khi kisi ne na ke diya to! Job achi nhi mili to me fail hu ghar pr maa- papa ne data to! Bas iske age kuch soch hi nhi pate. Me jb bahar sdko pr rhte hue logo ko, vriddhashram Or anathalayon ko dekhti hu to sochti hu jo log suicide attempt krte h kya un logo ka dukh in logo se bda hota hoga? In logo k pas khane ko dhang ka khana nhi, pehne ko kapde nhi, rhne ko chhat nhi, fir bhi umeed k sath jeete h aj nhi to kl sb acha hoga. Fir hm kyu nhi soch skte h yesa, kya kbhi socha h ki tumhare bad tumhare apno ka kya hoga?

Suppose hm family k eklote earning member huye to kya hoga, apne parents ke eklote child huye to tumhari las dekh kr un pr kya bitegi. Marna asan hota h jeena bhot mushkil to muskil kamo se dar jana kha ki smjhdari h.

Simple funda h jo life me apply krne jesa h lado jb tk lad sako 1 bar, 2bar, 3bar, 99bar haroge 100vi bar to jitoge tb sahi mayne ne zindaadili kehlaoge.

Priyanka Rawat

Name - Priyanka rawat(priya)
Place - bageshwar, Uttarakhand
Education - B.A
Hobbies - writing, skitching

कारण कुछ भी हो मुझे साथ चाहिए तुम्हारा
हुई जो थोड़ी नाराज तुमसे
न जाने क्यों नहीं हो रहा अब सवेरा
ना की बात कई दिनों से तुमसे
बेवजह खफ़ा है इतने दिनों से
भूल गए क्या वो पल जो साथ मे बिताये थे
पहले भी नाराज हुई मैं,पर तुम ने मनाया था
क्या यही है वो प्यार जो तुमने जताया था
हो जो मैं अलग क्या रह पाओगे तुम
मेरी बातों को याद कर क्या मुस्कुरा पाओगे तुम

Mampi Gayen

Mampi Gayen Lives in Kolkata Student of BA 2nd year
English as subjectWriting poem as a passion

The Oak Tree

My dear Oak tree I can't deny....
You're like the dazzling star in my life's empty sky.
When the tree was planted in my courtyard
I couldn't even expect that it closely attached with my heart.
I'd tried to recover your sweet love that I knew
My old, past childhood memories were incomplete without you.
All the day around you're become an open stage
Where Cuckoos and Baboons by their singing created a splendid image.
It stood tall, strong and proud like a giant
Its tranquility everytime attracted my mind.
You sheltered to many helpless

This was the precious memory that I couldn't erase.
My face was glittering in the sunshine
When I played on a swing made of your vine.
I'd seen life changing colour from moment to moment
But you never changed; you're alike till the end.

Dia Dey

Diya is an Indian girl. She is good writer and poet as well. She loves to write poems, Articles, Qoutes, Shayaris etc. She is passionate writer. She always work to write something different. Her hobby is to write poems and articles. She wants to do something big in future through her writing skills.

Just Know Me....

I understand you
But I can't stop my self to chase you
I don't know why you don't understand me
But you know why I like you
Because you never make me upset
You never feel me bad
You are always with me
Every time I miss you .....
 You are my priority

Muskan

Muskan from Bihar , completed my   10th from ABR foundation school and
Pursuing my further studies from Bal Vikas Vidyalaya .
I have been awarded for being a co - author abd a debater ..
Insta:- kuchhshayranaandaj

It's Today

Your beauty doesn't matters,
Your rationality does caters.
A dark world has evolved,
You will have to be brightly soared.
Time has brought you to the practical
 race,
Many hurdles you will face .
No doubt you will fall ,
But the time does justice hanging on the
 wall.
Many emotions and relations you will pay , And that would
only bring you as a   shining ray .
So don't be late ,
Find firmness in yourself merely as your
soulmate .

Love Has Lost The Love

Now love tends to find seductivity,
It is left with nothing but notoriety.
To teenagers it means daily talk,
To adults it means regular restraunt walk. Indeed love has
lost the love.
Alas! They are loving each other,
A child comments to amorous seen in
a picture.
Oh! This much love is dirty to him,
I am amazed at how the love is seen.
Indeed love has lost the love.
Before devotion was said as it's pen
name,
Now it's just a game.
Before it took long time fight,
But today it happens at first sight.
Oh! , indeed love has lost the love.

R.V.Teena

R.V.Teena, from Bikaner, Rajasthan   Completed her postgraduation from mgsu, Bikaner.

Writing is her ambition and even her passion. She like to express her feelings in words which are not said to people.

She love to be a part of anthologies and even her name in books,

Her writing inspiration is her father and full support by her mother on this way.

In future she want to see herself as an inspirable writer....

क्या था मेरा गुनाह??

(हवस का शिकार हुई लड़की की कहानी)
लड़की हूं इस बात का गर्व महसूस करूं   या बस
नाम के लिए लड़की हूं
इस बात पर फ़िक्र करूं
हां बहुत बड़े बड़े सपने संजोए थे
मगर सपनों को पूरा करने की राह
में हैवान मिल गए
छीनकर किताबे मेरी
मेरे शरीर पर अपने गंदे इरादे पूरे कर लिए
क्या ख्वाहिश थी मेरी बस यही कि
मैं खुद की पहचान बना लू
मगर इन हैवानों ने तो मार डाली मेरी रूह
फिर क्यूं डर गए अपने नाम खराब होने से
लूटकर मेरी आबरू
क्यू नही सोचा मेरे सपनो से जुड़ी
मेरे पापा की खुशियां
क्यों फाड़कर जला दी मेरे सपनो की निशानी
ऐसा भी क्या गुनाह कर दिया लड़की का जन्म लेकर
जो एक पल में ही ख़तम कर दी
अपनी मर्दानगी के खोखले दिखावे में
मेरी छोटी सी जिंदगानी

कोई अपना

ये पहचान अब बस शब्दों से चाहिए..
किसी का प्यार नहीं,
कोई बिना शर्त के साथ दे ऐसा साथी चाहिए..
लिखना महज शब्द नहीं,
 खुद की भावनाए हैं..
कोई समझ जाए मेरी भावनाएं
अब बस ऐसा कोई ज़िन्दगी चाहिए...
बेशक तनहा रहने लगे है सबके बीच,
पर कोई भीड़ में भी मुझे ढूंढ ले
अब बस ऐसा कोई अपना चाहिए ...
अब बस ऐसा कोई अपना चाहिए ।

Gunwanti Harish

Gunwanti Harish (Sonu)A girl with lot of dreams, and a passion to prove herself,Still a student, trying to make her dreams true.Born in Rajasthan.Science student, an upcoming writer.She likes to write what she feels, and loves to do what she wants to rather than thinking about the world's saying.She is a friend who is always to help people when they need her, even they are her enemies.She loves to listen music, and has very less friends.Her world is her mom and she loves her the most.You can connect with her at her Instagram @strings_of_heart7

जिदंगी..

ज़िन्दगी के हर मौके का फायदा उठाओ,
मगर किसी के भरोसे का नही,
जीवन में जितना चाहो मुस्कुराओ,
मगर किसी को रुला के नही,
चाहो तो छू लो तुम इस आसमान को,
मगर किसी को नीचे गिरा के नही,
तारे बन कर रोशन कर दो इस आसमाँ को,
मगर अँधेरा बनकर किसी को डराना नही,
फूल बनकर महका दो इस जहां को,
मगर काटे बनकर किसी को चुभना नही।।
थक गई थी..
शायद थोड़ा थक गई थी,
तो दूर निकलना छोड़ दिया,
पर ऐसा नहीं की मैने,
चलना ही छोड़ दिया,
फासले अक्सर रिश्तों में,
दूरिया बढा देते है,
पर ऐसा नहीं की मैने,
दोस्तो से मिलना छोड़ दिया,
हां ज़रा अकेली हु,
दुनिया की इस भीड़ में,
पर ऐसा नहीं की मैने,
दोस्ती निभाना छोड़ दिया।।

Somya Jain

Somya Jain
19 years old
Delhi

Apna Le Kali Ka Roop Tu

अपना ले काली का रूप तू
अब सीता का वक़्त नहीं
उठा ले शस्त्र तू
अब यहां कोई राम नहीं
कैंडल मार्च करते रह जाएंगे
साल बस यूंही बीत जाएंगे
ना आयेगी इंसाफ की घड़ी
टूट जाएगी तेरी रूह भी
रूठ जाएगा खुदा भी
ना मिलेगी किसी को सजा
ना मिलेगा तेरे रूह को सुकून
मत कर ऐतबार अब किसी पर तू
की अपना ले काली का रूप तू
ना देख सके तुझे कोई आंख उठा कर
बन जा इतनी कठोर तू
ज़िंदा दफना दे हर उस हेवान को
जिसकी नियत हो तुझ पे बिगड़े
की अपना ले काली का रूप तू
की अब सीता का वक़्त नहीं....!!!

Poonam B. Naik

poonam Naik is 20 year old B.Sc.B.Ed student at Ganpat Parsekar College of Education Harmal Goa. she is from Panjim City of Goa. Recently she have started writing poems in that she likes to write based on her daily life experience..

Hope

Hey my sunshine , why are you upset
You have a beautiful life,
so enjoy each step.
Don't think about your past and
Don't worry about your future.
Keep a faith in God and
believe in yourself..
I know it's too hard
When someone broke the magical heart..
but never loose your hope and
Heal the broken heart..
Hey my sunshine, just open your eyes
and try to see the fire flies
as they light during the night..
Similarly , you also see your positive site..
and try to fight with your dark night...

Nancy Chaudhary

I'm Nancy Chaudhary
I'm 19 years old. I belong
From- Burhar ,Sahdol (M.P).
I'm student of Bsc nurshing and I love write
Poem,Quote,Poet.

Mohabbat

Dhup ki chubhti kirno me chhao sa lgte ho ..
Sayad Mohabbat se lgte ho ..
Banjar si jamino me barish ja barste ho
PTA Ni kyo mohabbat se lgte ho ..
Dhadkan bn KR Dil Mai dhakte ho
Bs tum mohabbat se lgte ho ..
Anshu bn KR ankho se chhalkte ho
Ha tum mohabbat se lgte ho ...

Darshna Karushnaji Gaudkhede

I am darshna krushnaji gaurkhede from katol (district) Nagpur. And my age is 21 year.
I am pursuing education from G H Raisoni academy of engineering and technology nagpur in civil engineering 4 th year.

Duniya mai kuch aise rishte bhi hote h
Jin ke sry ya ty khane se
Chehre pe halki si muskan aa jati h!

Jindgi mai ab koi hasarat adhuri na rhi

"suno meri jan"

Tujhko pa liya ab jine ki aas nhi rhi

Flairs and Glairs, a platform by a student for the students. We are esteemed youth struggling to carve out our path for our future and we follow a basic mindset Since everyone is not born with all-round skills. Joining hands with people who are born to execute it with perfection is the best way to evolve. Self-Evolution is the need of the hour but, evolving as a community is what we strive for. The initiative as kickstarted by, Founder- Mr. Shubham Shah with the motive to utilize the skillset and talent of writing has now a team of 10+ people who are actively participating into newer forms of learning and discovering talents among youngsters. We Provide platform and services like Publishing opportunities, Open mics, Workshops, Hands-on training. Operating with Brand Name of Flairs and Glairs (Publication House), we offer the chance of elevating a passionate writer to an esteemed author With Brand name Teekhe Zasbaaat. We bring to you an opportunity to get accustomed with the Public Speaking and Presenting of Thoughts along with regular challenges to brush up your inking spirit. The newest initiative to extend our services we introduced in a new writing Platform- The Glittering Fables and Ink Over Tears.

We Choose to Fly Like A Falcon than to be

a Leg Pulling Crab.

To Know More: Infoline – 7781900870
Mail Us At-
flairsandglairs@gmail.com / info@flairsandglairs.in
Or Visit is at
www.flairsandglairs.com / www.flairsandglairs.in
Social Handles- @flairsandglairs @teekhezasbaaat

www.ingramcontent.com/pod-product-compliance
Lightning Source LLC
Chambersburg PA
CBHW071916120726
48001CB00005B/1760